STERLING CHILDREN'S BOOKS
New York

An Imprint of Sterling Publishing
387 Park Avenue South
New York, NY 10016

© 2013 by Sterling Publishing Co., Inc.
Design by Jennifer Browning

ISBN 978-1-4027-8336-4

Library of Congress Cataloging-in-Publication Data Available

Distributed in Canada by Sterling Publishing
c/o Canadian Manda Group, 165 Dufferin Street
Toronto, Ontario, Canada M6K 3H6
Distributed in the United Kingdom by GMC Distribution Services
Castle Place, 166 High Street, Lewes, East Sussex, England BN7 1XU
Distributed in Australia by Capricorn Link (Australia) Pty. Ltd.
P.O. Box 704, Windsor, NSW 2756, Australia

For information about custom editions, special sales, and premium and corporate
purchases, please contact Sterling Special Sales at 800-805-5489
or specialsales@sterlingpublishing.com.

Printed in China
Lot #:
2 4 6 8 10 9 7 5 3 1
01/13

www.sterlingpublishing.com/kids

SILVER PENNY STORIES

The Little Mermaid

Told by Deanna McFadden
Illustrated by Ashley Mims

The sea king, his six daughters, and their grandmother all lived in a beautiful castle made of coral, deep under the sea.

The littlest mermaid loved to hear about the world above the sea. She asked her grandmother to tell her stories about the ships, towns, and people.

The little mermaid spent many nights longing to see the moon and the stars clearly—not blurred through the surface of the sea.

"When you turn fifteen," her grandmother said, "you can rise to the surface and see the sky for yourself."

When her sisters grew up, they all swam to the surface of the sea. They returned and told the little mermaid stories of the world above.

At last, it was the little mermaid's fifteenth birthday. Her grandmother braided pearls into her hair and said, "You are all grown up now."

Light as a bubble, the little mermaid rose to the water's edge, where she saw a large ship. She heard music as she swam closer. A handsome young prince, also celebrating a birthday, stood on deck.

Suddenly, the sky rumbled. Lightning struck and rain fell. The ship tossed and turned and then it broke into pieces. The prince fell from the deck and sank into the water.

He must not die! the little mermaid thought. She swam to him and brought him back up to the air.

All night they drifted until they came to land. She placed his body on the beach very tenderly, and she began to swim away.

A crowd gathered around the prince. The little mermaid hid behind a rock and watched as people carried him away.

Back at home, she told her sisters all about the boat, the storm, and the prince.

"I know that prince!" her eldest sister said. "Come with me, I'll show you his castle."

She led the little mermaid to the prince's castle. It was perched on a cliff near the shore. The little mermaid spent hours floating below his window. The more time she spent watching the prince, the more she wanted to live in his world.

The little mermaid returned home and asked her grandmother if mermaids ever became human.

Her grandmother said, "Only at a great cost. You would lose your tail and never be able to live in the sea again."

The little mermaid loved her tail, her home, and her family, but she longed to live above the sea.

So, the little mermaid went to see an old witch in a dark part of the ocean.

"This potion will turn your tail into legs," the old witch said. "But be warned! You must make the prince fall in love with you. He must marry you and not another, or the potion will turn you into sea foam."

As payment, the witch took the little mermaid's voice. Just before the sun rose, the little mermaid swam to the same beach where she had left the prince.

She drank the potion quickly. The mermaid felt a splitting pain, but when it was gone, she looked down. Instead of a tail, she had two legs!

The prince found her on the shore. "Who are you?" he asked, but the little mermaid could not answer. Still, the prince found her eyes to be kind, and he invited her to walk with him.

He told her all about the terrible shipwreck and the girl from the sea who saved his life. The little mermaid longed to tell him that she was the girl from the sea.

Soon the prince and the little mermaid became great friends.

"You are so dear to me," the prince said to her. "Even though you cannot speak, I feel as if we are the closest of friends."

He told her everything—even that he was engaged to a princess from a faraway land.

The little mermaid wished she could change his mind, but she could not tell the prince how much she loved him.

The day of the prince's wedding arrived. The little mermaid kissed him good-bye and shed a tear. She knew that the witch's potion would turn her into sea foam.

The bells rang out in celebration of the wedding. But instead of turning into sea foam, the little mermaid began to float up into the air.

What is happening to me?
she wondered.

The daughters of the air answered her. "We are saving you from turning into sea foam," they said. "We have seen that you are good and kind. You may live with us forever as a spirit in the sky." And they continued to carry the little mermaid up into the air. Her heart swelled with joy.

Sometimes the little mermaid would look down at the castle where the prince lived. She would remember the happy time they had together. Sometimes she would think about her family in the sea. But most days and nights she played in the sky with the daughters of the air, for she was one of them now.